Pirate Trouble

Look out for more
mermaid adventures:
Spooky Shipwreck
Treasure Hunt
Whale Rescue

Mermaid Rock

Pirate Trouble

Kelly McKain
illustrated by Cecilia Johansson

Scholastic Canada Ltd.

Toronto New York London Auckland Sydney
Mexico City New Delhi Hong Kong Buenos Aires

To Millie, love Kelly

Scholastic Canada Ltd.
604 King Street West, Toronto, Ontario M5V 1E1, Canada

Scholastic Inc.
557 Broadway, New York, NY 10012, USA

Scholastic Australia Pty Limited
PO Box 579, Gosford, NSW 2250, Australia

Scholastic New Zealand Limited
Private Bag 94407, Greenmount, Auckland, New Zealand

Scholastic Children's Books
Euston House, 24 Eversholt Street, London NW1 1DB, UK

Library and Archives Canada Cataloguing in Publication
McKain, Kelly
Pirate trouble / Kelly McKain ; illustrated by Cecilia Johansson.
(Mermaid rock)
ISBN 0-439-93537-7 (pbk.)
I. Johansson, Cecilia II. Title. III. Series.
PR6113.C43P47 2007   j823'.92   C2006-903934-8

ISBN-10 0-439-93537-7 / ISBN-13 978-0-439-93537-1

First published in the UK by Scholastic Ltd., 2003.
First Canadian edition published 2007 by Scholastic Canada Ltd.

Text copyright © Kelly McKain, Prospero Promotions Limited, 2003.
Illustrations copyright © Cecilia Johansson, 2003.
All rights reserved.

6 5 4 3 2 1   Printed in Singapore   07 08 09 10 11

☆ Chapter One ☆

Spirulina wriggled around on Mermaid Rock. Barnacles were digging into her beautiful blue-green tail. "Being a mermaid is so boring," she grumbled.

Coralie and Shelle, her two sisters, tried to ignore her.

"Oh, Spirulina, do sit still," said Coralie bossily.

"But my tail's sore," Spirulina said grumpily. "It's stupid to sit on a jaggedy craggedy rock all day. We could be splashing around in the sea!"

"Yuck! Seawater messes up my hair," said Shelle, shocked.

"You two can sit there preening
yourselves and getting tail ache if you like,"
Spirulina told her sisters, "but I've got more
important things to do."

"Like what?" asked Shelle.

"I'm going to be a pirate," said Spirulina.

Coralie and Shelle laughed daintily.
"You? A pirate?"

"Yes, me," huffed Spirulina. "I'm going to build a pirate ship and sail the seven seas!"

"But you're only a little mermaid," giggled Coralie. "You're not brave enough."

"I am! You'll see!" cried Spirulina, sticking her tongue out at them. And with that she flicked her tail and dived into the sparkling sea.

☆ ☆ ☆

All morning Spirulina collected pieces of driftwood. Then she set about hammering and sawing and nailing them together to make a pirate ship.

She found an old shirt that had blown off the beach and used it as a sail.

"I name this ship the SS *Spirulina*!" she cried in delight.

"That silly boat will sink in a moment," called Coralie from Mermaid Rock.

"That sail's too tattered to hold the wind," shouted Shelle. "You won't get anywhere."

Spirulina frowned.
What if Coralie and
Shelle were right?
What if the SS *Spirulina*
did sink? What if the
sail was too tattered?

Suddenly a strong wind blew up and the
little boat began to skim away over the
ocean. Spirulina laughed with delight.

"Anchors aweigh!" she
called, tying on her
pirate headscarf.
"I'm afloat, me
shivering sisters!
I'm a-sailing away to adventures on the high
seas! I'll see you later!"

There was plenty to do on board the
pirate ship. Spirulina tickled a trout...

...juggled some jellyfish...

...and danced
with dolphins.

She swashbuckled
with seals...

...and sang sea
shanties.

At lunchtime, she took out her seaweed sandwiches and shared

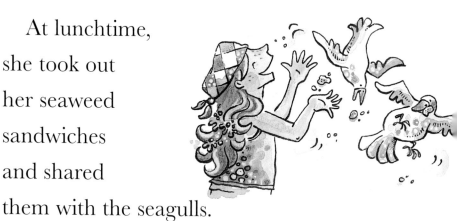

them with the seagulls.

Spirulina yawned. "It's hard work being a pirate," she said sleepily. "I think I'll curl up here on the deck for a snooze."

As the waves gently rocked her boat, Spirulina fell fast asleep. She didn't know it, but she was in terrible danger.

☆ Chapter Two ☆

Splish! Splash! Splosh!

Spirulina was woken by drops of rain falling on to her face.

She sat up with a start and stared around in horror. She had drifted far out to sea! She couldn't see Mermaid Rock any more. In fact, she couldn't see anywhere any more!

"Pirates don't panic," she told herself firmly. "I'll just set sail and hope that the shore comes into view."

But then disaster struck. Black storm clouds gathered above Spirulina's little boat. *Crackle-crackle-SNAP!* Lightning lit the stormy sky. *Rumble-rumble-BOOM!* Thunder rolled around her.

Then the rain lashed down. A fierce wind whipped Spirulina's hair and face. Wild waves battered her little boat. She clung to the mast as the SS *Spirulina* began to sink.

"Oh, what will I do?" she cried. "Lost in thunder and lightning! Sinking in a storm!" Two fat tears rolled down her face. "Coralie and Shelle were right," she sniffled. "I'm not brave enough to be a pirate!"

With that, she began to sob and sob. In fact, she was crying so hard that she almost missed the blurry shape on the horizon. She wiped her eyes and squinted through the rain.

"A ship!" she cried. "Thank goodness! Over here! Over here!"

The ship came closer...

...and closer...

...until it was right beside Spirulina's boat.

"Pirates!" gasped Spirulina.

A bearded man leaned over the side of the mighty galleon.

"Ahoy there!" he bellowed. "What have we here? Shipmate Shifty, come and look at this!"

A pink-faced man appeared. "That's a little lost mermaid, Captain Curly," he said.

"We were just going your way, me little mer-mate," roared Captain Curly. "Climb aboard and bring your vessel. We'll take you home."

Spirulina wasn't sure whether she could trust the pirates…but she didn't have any choice. "Thank you," she called.

Captain Curly helped her aboard the pirate ship.

☆ Chapter Three ☆

"Pretty Polly!"

Spirulina whirled round. She saw a parrot in a cage swinging from the rigging.

"Pretty Polly!" the parrot squawked again.

"Shut up, Polly," snarled Captain Curly. "You're not a Pretty Polly, you're a scrawny old bird!"

Spirulina looked
at the parrot.
Its eyes were sad
and its feathers
were falling off.

"Pretty Polly!" it squawked again.

"That parrot's driving me mad," roared
Captain Curly. "Bony Bosun, throw it in the
brig!"

"Aye, aye, Captain!" Bony Bosun took the
parrot cage and threw it into the brig.

"That's not a nice way to treat a parrot," cried Spirulina, but the pirates ignored her.

"Hey, little lost mermaid," bellowed Captain Curly, "show us some mermaiding."

"Aye, sing us a tune, go on," called Bony Bosun.

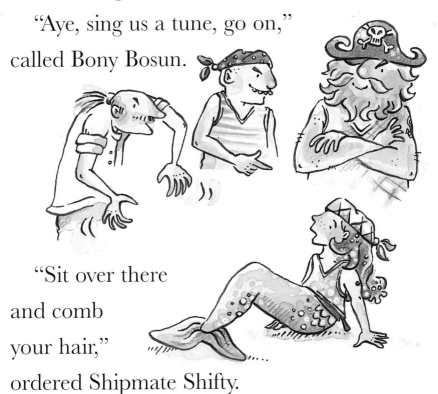

"Sit over there and comb your hair," ordered Shipmate Shifty.

"I'm not that kind of mermaid," said Spirulina crossly. "I sail the seven seas and have adventures and – "

"Ha, ha, ha!" roared the pirates. "Well, if you're not going to do what a mermaid should, then we'll have to lock you up with that silly parrot!"

Then Bony Bosun picked Spirulina up,
tossed her into the brig and turned the key.

"That's not a nice way to treat a
mermaid!" shouted Spirulina.

But the pirates just roared with laughter.
Captain Curly tapped his wooden leg on
the deck. "Come on, lads! Let's sleep here
until the storm has passed. Then we'll put
our wicked plan into action!"

Spirulina gulped. What wicked plan?

"Those pirates are really terrible," sighed Spirulina.

"I agree!" squawked the parrot.

Spirulina stared at it, amazed. "But, Polly," she cried, "I thought you could only say 'Pretty Polly'."

"That's all I ever say to them," said the parrot smugly. "It really drives them crazy! And besides, my name's not Polly, it's Jennifer."

"Nice to meet you, Jennifer," said Spirulina. "I'm Spirulina."

"How do you do?" squawked Jennifer. "It's lovely to have someone sensible to talk to at last. I hate being stuck in this horrible cage. That's why all my feathers are falling off."

"I can help you," said Spirulina. She pulled a pair of pliers from her tool belt and pried the bars of the cage apart.

Jennifer tottered out and stretched
her wings.

"Ah, that's better," she sighed happily.
"Thank you,
Spirulina."

Spirulina grinned. "Now all we have to
do is escape and find out what
those wicked pirates are
up to."

"I know what they're up to," squawked Jennifer. "They're sailing to Mermaid Rock, to steal the purses of those two preening mermaids."

Spirulina gasped in horror. "Those two preening mermaids are my sisters Coralie and Shelle!" she exclaimed. "Oh, Jennifer, we've got to stop the pirates!"

☆ Chapter Four ☆

As the rain drummed down onto the brig,
Spirulina came up with a pirate-busting
plan, which she whispered to Jennifer.

"That's brilliant!" squawked Jennifer.
"But first we've got to get out of here!
I think I could squeeze through those
window bars and steal the keys."

They listened to check that the coast was clear.

Sure enough, the sound of snoozing pirates filled the air.

Jennifer breathed in, folded her wings and wriggled between two of the bars.

She flew across the deck and took the bunch of keys from the ring at Captain Curly's waist.

Then she zoomed back and set Spirulina free.

Spirulina crept out of the brig.

She sneaked around to the galley and found a huge vat of oil. Grinning, she poured the oil all along the deck and down the plank.

Next, she tipped the pirates' rum into the sea.

Then she filled up the jug with seawater and a couple of baby crabs.

Meanwhile, Jennifer set a trap with her cage.

Last of all, Spirulina took out her hammer and quietly tapped a nail into the bottom of Captain Curly's peg leg.

They just made it
back into the brig
before the
pirates
woke up.

"Land ahoy, me hearties!" Captain
Curly bellowed. "The storm has passed
and Mermaid Rock is straight ahead!"

When Coralie and Shelle spotted the
pirate ship they started
to scream.

"Surrender your purses, my lovelies,"
roared Captain Curly, "or prepare to feel
my silver cutlass on your pretty necks!"

"Yeah, hand 'em over," shouted Shipmate Shifty.

"Help! Help!" cried Coralie. "Wicked pirates are stealing our precious jewels!"

"Help! Help!" shrieked Shelle. "Someone save us!"

☆ Chapter Five ☆

Spirulina came dashing out of the brig.
"Spirulina to the rescue!" she cried.

"And Jennifer to the rescue too," squawked
the parrot, flapping along behind her.

"No mermaid gets the better of me!"
roared Captain Curly. He lunged towards
Spirulina, his silver cutlass flashing.

But he didn't get anywhere. The nail Spirulina had hammered into his peg leg pinned him to the deck! He was FURIOUS. "Get 'em, lads!" he bellowed.

Shipmate Shifty and Bony Bosun ran at Spirulina.

Bony Bosun slid on the oily deck – and fell straight into Jennifer's trap.

Jennifer tugged a rope and the cage lifted off the ground.

"Ha! See how you like it," she squawked, winching Bony Bosun up the rigging. He swung back and forth miserably, waving his skinny arms and legs.

Shipmate Shifty grabbed the rum jug and took a swig for courage.

"Pah!" He spat out salty seawater. "Ouch! Ouch!" Two tiny crabs pinched his nose tight.

"'Elp! 'Elp! Get 'em off!" He skidded madly round and round on the slippery deck.

"Waaaaaaaaaaaaah!" He shot past Spirulina, slid down the plank and fell headfirst into the sea.

Spirulina and
Jennifer
cheered as
Shipmate Shifty
spluttered
about in
the water...

...Bony Bosun swung
upside down in the
parrot cage...

...and Captain
Curly waved his
cutlass uselessly.

"Hooray!
We're saved!"
cried Coralie
and Shelle
in delight.

Spirulina leaped onto the SS *Spirulina* and
Jennifer gave her a push. The little boat
went skidding down the oily deck and
splashed into the sea – headed straight
for home.

With Jennifer on her shoulder, Spirulina scrambled onto Mermaid Rock. Coralie and Shelle clapped and cheered.

They all watched as the great pirate galleon sailed off into the ocean, with Shipmate Shifty swimming after it.

"You saved us, Spirulina," cried Coralie.

"You really are a brave adventurer!" said Shelle.

"It was Jennifer too," Spirulina insisted.

Jennifer shook her feathers in delight.

"Can I have a ride in your boat, Spirulina?" asked Coralie shyly.

"Can I wear your pirate headscarf?" asked Shelle.

"Of course," Spirulina replied, smiling.

They played pirates all afternoon in the sunshine. Coralie and Shelle got great big tangly knots in their hair. But they were having so much fun that they didn't care one bit.